First published in English by Greystone Books in 2022
Originally published in Spanish as *Formas de hacer amigos*
copyright © 2021 Leetra Final, S.A. de C.V., Mexico City
English translation copyright © 2022 by Elisa Amado

22 23 24 25 26   5 4 3 2 1

Greystone Kids / Greystone Books Ltd.
greystonebooks.com

An Aldana Libros book

Cataloguing data available from Library and Archives Canada
ISBN 978-1-77164-975-9 (cloth)
ISBN 978-1-77164-976-6 (epub)

Jacket design by Erika González and Jessica Sullivan
Interior design by Erika González

Printed and bound in Singapore on FSC® certified paper at
COS Printers Pte Ltd. The FSC® label means that materials used
for the product have been responsibly sourced.

Greystone Books gratefully acknowledges the Musqueam,
Squamish, and Tsleil-Waututh peoples on whose land our
Vancouver head office is located.

Greystone Books thanks the Canada Council for the Arts, the
British Columbia Arts Council, the Province of British Columbia
through the Book Publishing Tax Credit, and the Government of
Canada for supporting our publishing activities.

Ways to
Make
FRIENDS

Jairo Buitrago • Mariana Ruiz Johnson

Translated by Elisa Amado

AN ALDANA LIBROS BOOK

GREYSTONE KIDS

GREYSTONE BOOKS • VANCOUVER / BERKELEY / LONDON

To make friends
you should sit under a huge tree.

You will need to be very patient
and wait until someone comes along
who wants to be your friend.
But at least you won't get sunburned.
A leaf might even fall on your head.

When you are at your aunt's
house, you can free a bird.

It will fly far away very quickly,
and you might not see it again.
But it will always remember you.
It will be your friend.

If you find a bee splashing in a fountain,
help it out of the water using a little leaf.
Let it dry out in the sun and it will be so happy.

If it gets angry, because
sometimes bees can be bad tempered,
just run away. Anyway, what friend
doesn't get cranky sometimes?

This way you can go home
under that very same sun,
happy that you have made friends.

Sit on a park bench
and cut out paper dolls.
Leave them as presents
all over the place.

Say hi to the shy kid who never says hi to anyone. After you've said hi at least forty times, he might even say hi back, exactly like an old friend.

You can dress up like an
apple or a pear and give away
a pear or an apple.

Show someone how to make
shadow animals with your hands.
If you make a shadow in the shape
of an elephant, you can say hello
with the shadow trunk.

And when you are at the movies, you can talk about the movie with the neighbor on your left though you don't know her. You can even help yourself to some of her popcorn.

It works really well to make a phone out of a very, very long piece of string and two empty cups. You stand at one end and when your future friend answers, you can say,

"Hi! I'll meet you under the huge tree. I'll be disguised as an apple." That's how to arrange a meeting.

Being friends with a cactus can be
nice and calm and quiet, and you can also
take it for a walk in your wagon.

You need to remember that even if you
can't hug it and it doesn't have a lot to say,
it will keep all your secrets.

But if by late afternoon you get tired
of making friends, just be by yourself and forget
everything that this book has told you to do.

Drawing, reading, singing, shouting.
These are good ways to pass the time and
to learn to be your own best friend.

And at the end of the day,
you will see the light of the
sun disappear. It is night.

You will be happy and sleepy.
So will the cactus, though
it won't tell you so.

Printed on paper that has been responsibly sourced.
The illustrations were made with colored pens and digital color.

Friends were made in the making of this book.